**Education
Library Support for Schools
Victoria Buildings
Queen Street
Falkirk
FK2 7AF**

RE4
r
DAM

Falkirk Council

www.raintreepublishers.co.uk
Visit our website to find out
more information about
Raintree books.

To order:
Phone 0845 6044371
Fax +44 (0) 1865 312263
Email myorders@capstonepub.co.uk

Customers from outside the UK please telephone +44 1865 312262

Raintree is an imprint of Capstone Global Library Limited,
a company incorporated in England and Wales
having its registered office at 7 Pilgrim Street, London,
EC4V 6LB – Registered company number: 6695582

Text © Stone Arch Books 2010
First published in the United Kingdom
in hardback and paperback in 2010
The moral rights of the proprietor have been asserted.

Art Director: Kay Fraser
Graphic Designer: Hilary Wacholz
Production Specialist: Michelle Biedschied
Editor: Vaarunika Dharmapala
Originated by Capstone Global Library Ltd
Printed and bound in China
by South China Printing Company Ltd

ISBN 978 1 406215 19 9 (hardback)
14 13 12 11 10
10 9 8 7 6 5 4 3 2 1

ISBN 978 1 406215 33 5 (paperback)
14 13 12 11 10
10 9 8 7 6 5 4 3 2 1

British Library Cataloguing in Publication Data
A full catalogue record for this book is available
from the British Library.

CONTENTS

CHAPTER 1
THE HANGING TOOTH 5

CHAPTER 2
SNAIR ISLAND 11

CHAPTER 3
THE STONE HUT 16

CHAPTER 4
THE NARROW VALLEY 28

FANG FACTS 34
ABOUT THE AUTHOR AND ILLUSTRATOR 36
GLOSSARY 37
DISCUSSION QUESTIONS 38
WRITING PROMPTS 39

Introduction

A new Age of Dragons is about to begin. The powerful creatures will return to rule the world once more, but this time it will be different. This time, they will have allies who will help them. Around the world, some young humans are making a strange discovery. They are learning that they were born with dragon blood – blood that gives them amazing powers.

CHAPTER 1
THE HANGING TOOTH

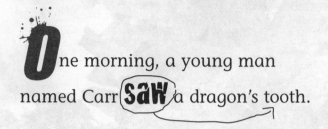

One morning, a young man named Carr **saw** a dragon's tooth.

Carr was a scientist at a college in Scotland.

That **morning** he was on his way
to his lab.

Carr saw a young woman
wearing a necklace. A **STRANGE**,
curved stone hung below her neck.

"Excuse me," said Carr. "I like your **NECKLACE**."

"Oh, thanks," said the young woman.

"May I ask where you got that?" Carr asked.

The woman smiled. "My boyfriend made it," she said.

She held it out for Carr to see.

"He found the stone on **Snair Island**," she said.

"He was on holiday there with some friends."

The young woman smiled and then **hurried** away to her lesson.

Carr stood there, amazed.

He had **recognized** the stone hanging from the necklace.

It was NOT a stone. It was a tooth. A **DRAGON'S** tooth.

CHAPTER 2
SNAIR ISLAND

The island was rocky and covered with steep, **jagged** hills. It had one lonely village.

Carr visited the village shops and talked with people.

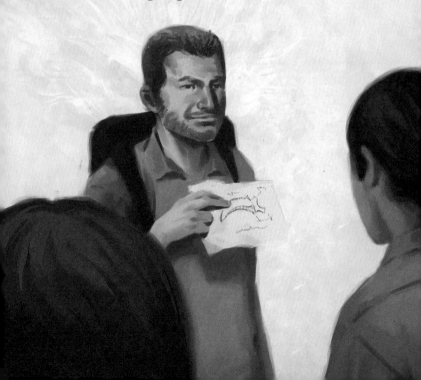

He showed them a drawing of the dragon tooth.

"Have you seen anything like this?" Carr asked them.

The village people shook their heads.

They did **NOT** understand what Carr was talking about.

Finally, Carr visited a small, **DUSTY** bookshop.

The owner listened carefully to Carr and nodded his bald head.

"Yes, I have seen a stone like that before," he said. "Many of them. You can find them up in the hills."

Carr thanked the old man and left the bookshop.

Through his **window,** the owner
watched Carr walk down the street.

There was **FEAR** in the old
man's eyes.

CHAPTER 3
THE STONE HUT

Carr rented a van and drove up into the hills.

The road was **rough** and full of holes.

An hour later, **high** in the hills, the road ended.

Carr had to get out and **walk.**

The sun was **beginning** to set when **Carr** saw a small stone hut.

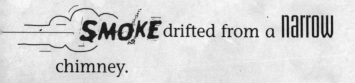 **SMOKE** drifted from a **narrow** chimney.

Carr knocked at the **wooden** door. A boy opened it. He looked ~ surprised. ~

"Come in," said the boy.

In the hut's main room was a fireplace.

A thin, red-haired woman sat warming herself by the **fire**.

Carr **explained** that he was a scientist.

He had come to **Snair Island** to study the rocks.

Then he showed them a picture of the dragon tooth.

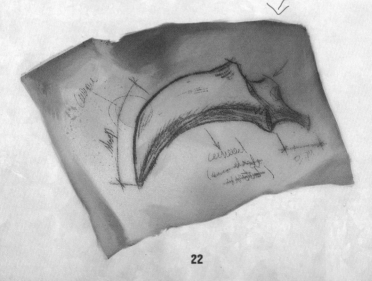

The boy's eyes grew **wide**.

He looked at the woman and then back at Carr. The woman nodded.

"Yes," she said. "Jamie can show you tomorrow."

Then she and the boy **invited** Carr to eat with them. They did not have much food, but they gave Carr the **BIGGEST** helping.

That **night**, the woman and Jamie slept in front of the fire.

They gave Carr the hut's **only** bed to sleep in. He slept in a tiny room behind the fireplace.

It was **midnight** when a noise woke Carr. He looked out of the bedroom's small window.

Outside, above the trees, flew a giant **shadow** with wings.

Then Carr saw another, smaller shadow. It turned **somersaults** in the starry sky.

The **HUGE** wings flapped and beat against the air. The scientist smiled.

CHAPTER 4
THE NARROW VALLEY

The next morning, Jamie led Carr higher into the hills.

They came to a **DARK**, narrow valley. Smooth cliffs rose on either side.

The boy seemed to be searching the **ground**.

Carr began to **stare** at the ground too.

"Here!" shouted Jamie.

He was holding (something) in his hand.

A **tooth!**

"Yes," said Carr, excited. "That's what I was hoping to find."

Carr noticed **BLOOD** on the end of the tooth.

This is **fresh**, he thought.

Carr smiled and looked down
at Jamie.

The boy smiled back.

One of his teeth was missing.

FANG FACTS

Most children start losing their teeth around 6 or 7 years of age. They often place the lost tooth under a pillow for the tooth fairy. Centuries ago, there were other ways to dispose of a lost tooth.

* In England, many mothers burned the teeth. This prevented a witch from getting the tooth and using it to place a curse on the child.

* Ancient Egyptians would throw the teeth up towards the sun.

* In Europe, parents would bury the tooth. They did this for two reasons: to ensure the growth of a new tooth, and to protect the children from witches.

* VIKINGS gave children a tooth fee in exchange for their baby teeth.

Today, people wear shark tooth necklaces for fashion. But men in Hawaii have worn them since early times to protect them from evil.

An average person has **32** teeth – eight incisors, four canines, twelve molars, and eight pre-molars.

The **enamel** on your teeth is the hardest thing in your body. It is even harder than bone.

Teeth start growing six months before birth.

One in every 2,000 babies is born with a tooth already showing.

ABOUT THE AUTHOR

Michael Dahl is the author of more than 200 books for children and young adults. He has won the AEP Distinguished Achievement Award three times for his non-fiction. His Finnegan Zwake mystery series was shortlisted twice by the Anthony and Agatha awards. He has also written the Library of Doom series. He is a featured speaker at conferences on graphic novels and high-interest books for boys.

ABOUT THE ILLUSTRATOR

After getting a graphic design degree and working as a designer for a couple of years, Federico Piatti realized he was spending far too much time drawing and painting, and too much money on art books and comics, so his path took a turn towards illustration. He currently works creating imagery for books and games, mostly in the fantasy and horror genres.

GLOSSARY

chimney upright pipe that carries smoke out of a house

hut small, basic house

jagged uneven and sharp

lab short for laboratory, a room containing special equipment for people to use in experiments

narrow not broad or wide

recognize see and understand something

rough not smooth

scientist person who studies nature and the physical world

somersault tucking one's head into one's chest and rolling in a complete circle

steep sharply sloping up or down

valley area of low ground between hills

DISCUSSION QUESTIONS

1. Why did Carr want one of the dragon teeth?

2. What do you think about Jamie and his mum? Were they good **people** or bad? Talk about your answer.

3. Where did the **TOOTH** come from that Jamie gave to Carr?

WRITING PROMPTS

1. Imagine that you are a **young** dragon. Write a letter to a friend describing the adventures you have.

2. In this book, Jamie lives with his mother. **Choose** one of the people you live with to write about. What is that person like?

3. What do you think **happens** after this book ends? Write a chapter that extends the story.

FALKIRK COUNCIL
LIBRARY SUPPORT
FOR SCHOOLS

MORE BOOKS TO READ

LIBRARY OF DOOM

Meet the mysterious Librarian. Keeper of the world's most dangerous books, sworn enemy of monsters made of paper and ink, crusader of young people threatened by ancient curses... Enter the Library of Doom to follow these heart-pounding adventures.